SOWN
AMONGST THORNS

**GOODBYE WORLD
I STAY NO LONGER
WITH YOU**

**IN MEMORY OF A GOOD
FRIEND
ARWINDER SINGH**

STORY BY:

GEORGE OKUEFUNA

ART BY:

GEORGE OKUEFUNA

JOSE 'ZITIS' PAOLO

OLABODE .S. AJIBOYE

MUTRI KARYA

EDITED BY

KATHY NGUYEN

Dedicated to the pursuit
of the dream

Sacrificing who you are
for what you will become

Wanting to succeed as
bad as you wanna
breathe.

Eric Thomas

Special Thanks:

Christian Niteh - for dealing with all my BS, Mom, Big Sis, Obi Okeke, Ania Pzylblska, Ivaylo Ivanov and you for trying me out!

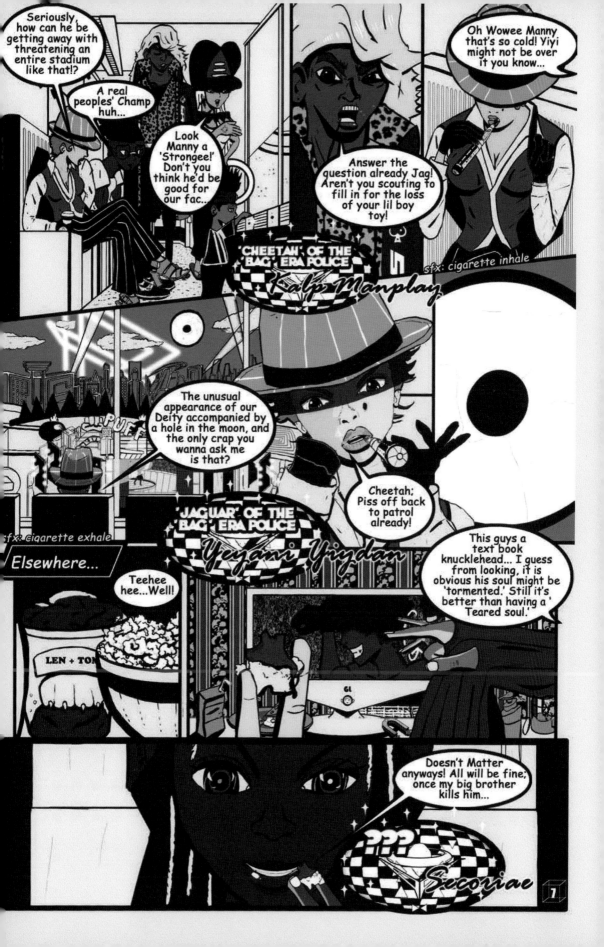

SOWN amongst THORNS

GEORGE OKUEFUNA

Former cover page...

16

CURTAIN CALL?

Looks like somebody enjoyed their read, I've been waiting this whole time to talk to you!

I'm Secoriae, you might have spotted me near the start of the story. Yeah I didn't get much airtime and at this rate that's all you see of me, Hibby, Iy, that woman on the page before and the rest of the cast, isn't that the biggest bummer!

Don't threat however as there's still hope! In order to continue the story, please support this comic by spreading the word of its' awesomeness to your friends by sharing the Sown Amongst Thorns link on Facebook! You can also follow us on Instagram @sown_amongst_thorns and subscribe to the Youtube Channel 'MoveLegacies' for updates.

Also Keep a lookout on Kickstarter for a campaign for the book to start around 1st September as well!

This is to be one hell of an adventure and our author is super on board to continue, he just needs some help that's all, so pretty please support us!

Whatever you do, I'd just like to say Thank You for reading Sown Amongst Thorns Issue #1. Don't forget to leave a positive review on Amazon and I hope to see you again for the bigger and more action packed issue #2!

Printed in Great Britain
by Amazon